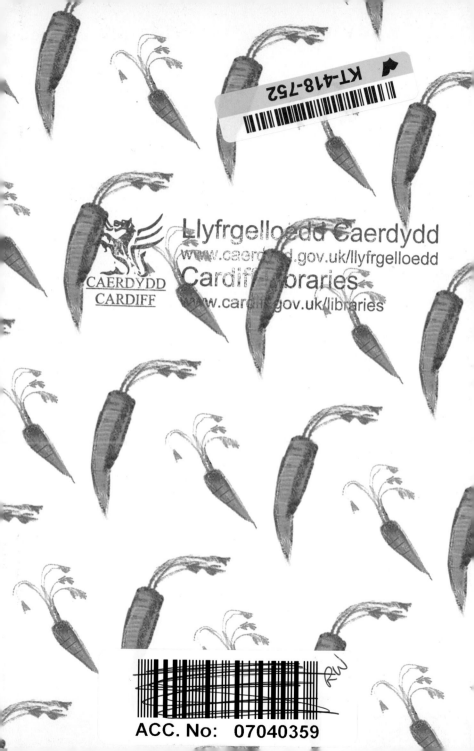

KT-418-752

Llyfrgelloedd Caerdydd
www.caerdydd.gov.uk/llyfrgelloedd
Cardiff Libraries
www.cardiff.gov.uk/libraries

CAERDYDD
CARDIFF

ACC. No: 07040359

Little Rabbit's Big Surprise

For Phoenix – Swapna

For Cal xxxx – Alison

STRIPES PUBLISHING LTD
An imprint of the Little Tiger Group
1 Coda Studios, 189 Munster Road, London SW6 6AW

First published in Great Britain in 2019

Text copyright © Swapna Haddow, 2019
Illustrations copyright © Alison Friend, 2019

ISBN: 978-1-78895-029-9

The right of Swapna Haddow and Alison Friend to be identified as
the author and illustrator of this work respectively has been asserted
by them in accordance with the Copyright, Designs and Patents Act, 1988.

All rights reserved.

A CIP catalogue record for this book is available from the British Library.

This book is sold subject to the condition that it shall not, by way of trade or otherwise, be lent,
resold, hired out, or otherwise circulated without the publisher's prior consent in any form of
binding or cover other than that in which it is published and without a similar condition including
this condition being imposed upon the subsequent purchaser.

Printed and bound in China.

STP/1800/0232/1118

2 4 6 8 10 9 7 5 3 1

Little Rabbit's Big Surprise

Swapna Haddow

Illustrated by Alison Friend

Stripes

This tale starts,
like good tales often do,
with a little rabbit.

This little rabbit is looking
for something to do.

"Play with me?" Little Rabbit said
as she tugged at her mama.

"Not now," Mama said.
"I have much too much to do."

"But I'm bored," Little Rabbit moaned.

"Ask your brothers and sisters," Mama said, gently placing Little Rabbit on the floor.

Little Rabbit looked around the warren she shared with her mother, her brothers and sisters and her grandfather.

The comfy burrow was filled with sunlight
and chatter as her brothers and sisters hurried
about getting on with their morning chores.

Little Rabbit sighed.
"They're all busy," she grumbled.

"How about calling on Little Mole and Little Hedgehog?" Mama suggested, clearing away the ends of the dandelion leaves from breakfast. "I'm sure Big Rabbit will take you."

Of course! Little Rabbit's best friends would surely want to play.

"Good idea," Little Rabbit said. She bounced out of the warren, calling out "bye Mama" and catching the kiss her mother blew to her.

Little Rabbit *loved* her home. As she hopped
out into the meadow on the edge of the
woodland, she took a deep breath in and caught
the sweet scent of the wildflowers.

She watched the busy bees collecting nectar
and tapped off the last drops of dew from the
tips of the long grass. Today was a perfect day
for playing hoppity hop with her friends.

"Big Rabbit," she called to her
grandfather, who was sitting
in the sun. "Can we go
and see Little Mole and
Little Hedgehog?"

"We could," he said, hopping over
to join his granddaughter. "But I saw
Little Mole and Little Hedgehog head off
early this morning to help Big Hedgehog
collect slugs and worms for dinner."

Little Rabbit screwed up her nose.
She loved being with her friends but
collecting worms wasn't much fun.

"I wish they were collecting carrots
instead." Little Rabbit sighed,
plonking herself down in a huff.
"Now who will I play with?"

"You can help me out,"
Big Rabbit offered.

"Help you out?" said Little Rabbit,
pulling at her long ears with her paws.
"With what?"

"I've got some work to do,"
her grandfather said, ruffling the
silky-soft fur on Little Rabbit's head.
"You can be my assistant."

"*Work?* But you don't have a job!"
Little Rabbit laughed. "You spend
all day with your friends."

Big Rabbit smiled. He lifted
Little Rabbit and swung her up
on to his shoulders.
"Why don't you spend
the day with me and see?"

"OK,"
Little Rabbit said,
"but only if we can
play a game."

"How about a game of I Spy?"
said Big Rabbit.

"I love that game," Little Rabbit squealed.

"I'll start, shall I?" Big Rabbit suggested.
"I spy with my little eye something
beginning with … T."

"Is it a tree?" Little Rabbit guessed.

"No."

"Of course not." Little Rabbit giggled.

She balanced herself on her grandfather's
shoulders, then leaped on to a tree stump.
"That's far too obvious."

"How about a **toadstool**?"
Little Rabbit asked.

She bounced from the
tree stump on to a
flat-headed toadstool.

"No," Big Rabbit said. "Not a toadstool."

The two rabbits hopped along the track where the meadow met the woodland, leaving a trail of paw prints in the soil.

"Is it a twisty twig? Tulips? Twittering birds?"

"No. No. And no."

"You've picked a difficult one, Big Rabbit," said Little Rabbit, dancing between her grandfather's paws.

"Do you need a clue?" he teased, his nose twitching towards something.

Little Rabbit's gaze followed Big Rabbit's wriggling nose in the direction of a little hill. She skipped ahead, trailing a small line of molehills and pointed to a mound of dirt.

"I know! Is it the Moles' tunnel?"

"Yes!" said Big Rabbit. "You got it,
Little Rabbit."

The rabbits hopped over and Big Rabbit
stamped his foot hard. "Hello? Is anyone in?"

A bright pink snout poked up
through the entrance of the tunnel.

"Greetings, Big Rabbit,"
said Mole, his brow furrowed.

"Is everything all right?" Big Rabbit asked.

Mole shook his head.
"It's a disaster. An utter disaster," he cried.

"I'm sure we can fix your disaster,"
said Big Rabbit calmly. He offered Mole
his paws. "Let me help you out."

Little Rabbit watched her grandfather help
Mole out of the tunnel. The entrance was so
dark that she stepped away from the soft soil
– one wrong foot and a rabbit could take
a nasty tumble into the darkness.

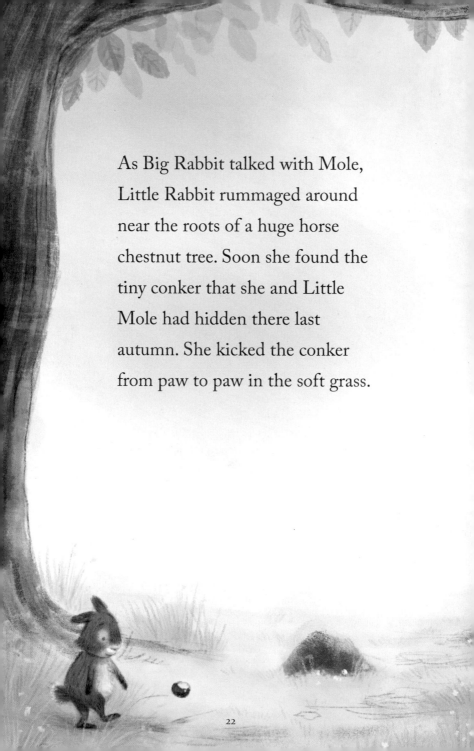

As Big Rabbit talked with Mole,
Little Rabbit rummaged around
near the roots of a huge horse
chestnut tree. Soon she found the
tiny conker that she and Little
Mole had hidden there last
autumn. She kicked the conker
from paw to paw in the soft grass.

"Is this your new burrow?" Big Rabbit asked.

Mole nodded. "But I didn't realize how much of a shadow the huge horse chestnut tree cast over the tunnel. Nobody wants to visit us because our burrow is too dark."

Big Rabbit blinked as he looked down into the hole. "Hmm, it is *particularly* dark."

"We wanted to have Little Mole's birthday party here," Mole continued, "but no one will come because it's too dark for the children to play safely."

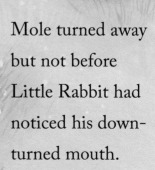

Mole turned away but not before Little Rabbit had noticed his down-turned mouth.

Big Rabbit patted his friend on
the shoulder. "Leave it to me, Mole.
I'll be back in the morning to make
sure Little Mole gets his party."

"Thank you, Big Rabbit,"
Mole said, waving goodbye to
the rabbits as they hopped away.

"Mole's really worried about those dark tunnels, isn't he?" Little Rabbit said.

Big Rabbit nodded. "It won't be much of a party if Little Mole's friends don't come."

"I wouldn't miss it for the world!" Little Rabbit exclaimed. "Little Mole's birthday parties are the best in the woodland."

"Don't worry, Little Rabbit," said Big Rabbit, taking her by the paw. "We'll find a way to help Mole and his family."

Her grandfather's big kind eyes made
Little Rabbit's worries disappear.

"Let's race to the hedgerow," Big Rabbit
said. "I've got to call on Granny Hedgehog."

The two rabbits leaped through the long grass. The sweet scent of primroses and bluebells wafted across the meadow. Little Rabbit could feel the wind in her fur as she chased after her grandfather, landing in his large footprints as she tried to keep up.

"You're getting fast, Little Rabbit,"
Big Rabbit panted.
"You almost beat me!"

They hurried towards a neatly
tended nest made of moss and leaves,
tucked beneath the hedgerow on
the far side of the meadow.

"Granny Hedgehog?"
Little Rabbit called out.

There was no reply.
This was most unlike
Granny Hedgehog.

"Granny Hedgehog?" Big Rabbit tried.

His ears stood up in alarm. There was none of the usual clatter as the elderly hedgehog made her way out of her nest and there was no familiar waft of spicy mushroom pie.

Finally he made out Granny Hedgehog's weak voice. "Come in, Big Rabbit," she said softly.

The rabbits hurried inside.

Granny sat wrapped up tight in a soft
moss blanket. Her nose was rosy red
and her cheeks were pale.

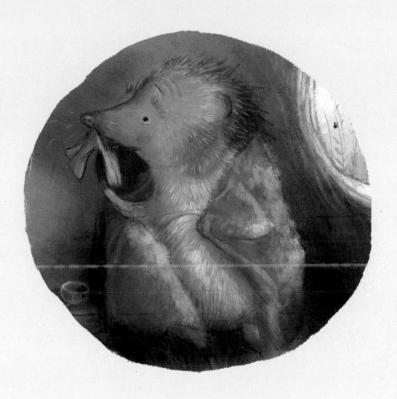

"Oh, Granny Hedgehog,"
Big Rabbit exclaimed.
"You don't look well at all!"

"It's just a cold," Granny replied
with a meek smile.
She sniffled and sneezed and then blew
her nose like an out-of-tune trumpet.

"Can we get you anything?"
asked Big Rabbit.

"I'll be fine," Granny said.

"I just need to rest and it will pass."

"We had a race to the hedgerow," Little
Rabbit said, eager to tell Granny Hedgehog
all about it. "I almost beat Big Rabbit."

"Is that so?" Granny smiled, the colour in her cheeks returning as she thought of the two rabbits racing in the sunshine. "Once I'm well, we'll have to see if you can beat me."

Big Rabbit smiled at his granddaughter
and poured out a fresh pot of hot berry tea.

"A story always makes me feel better when
I'm cooped up inside with a cold," Big Rabbit
said, picking up a book to read to Granny.

Granny Hedgehog snored softly as
Big Rabbit read the last line of the story
and gently placed the book on the table.

Little Rabbit followed in Big Rabbit's
footsteps as they tiptoed outside. As they
left the nest, Big Rabbit's nose twitched.
"I think we have some new neighbours."

Little Rabbit followed her grandfather's
gaze to just beyond the hedgerow.
A family of dormice were moving in.

They were greeted by four baby dormice,
all crying for their dad's attention as he
tried to build them a nest.

"I'm hungry!" two cried.
"I'm tired!" the other
two wailed.

"You look like you have your
paws full," Big Rabbit said,
picking up the tiniest of the babies.

The little dormouse stopped
snivelling and giggled as Big Rabbit
held her higher and higher.

"We've just moved in," the father said.
"I'm Dormouse."

"I'm Big Rabbit. And this is my
granddaughter, Little Rabbit."

Dormouse looked inside their new home and shook his head in dismay. "This nest isn't big enough for all of us," he sighed. "I need some more twigs to make it bigger."

Little Rabbit peered inside the nest. It was far too small for the whole family.

Dormouse scampered over to a nearby bin. He dug around inside and pulled out a shiny piece of paper. "This is no use at all," he grumbled.

"The best nest-building twigs are on the other side of the meadow, in the woodland," Big Rabbit called. "I could show you if you like."

As Dormouse scurried back, the babies grizzled and began to cry again.

"That's very kind but my babies are too little to be left on their own," Dormouse said, bouncing them one by one to cheer them up. "And I really must find some food."

His shoulders dropped at the thought of feeding his babies and building a bigger nest.

"You go and find food," Big Rabbit reassured Dormouse. "Little Rabbit and I will look after the children."

The rabbits entertained the dormice babies with stories and games. When Dormouse returned with his arms full of berries and nuts, the children grabbed hungrily at the food. Before long they were huddled in a contented heap.

As the rabbits said goodbye, Little Rabbit asked if she could have the shiny paper Dormouse had found earlier. "It would make a brilliant kite," she said. And Dormouse agreed.

Little Rabbit let out a big yawn.

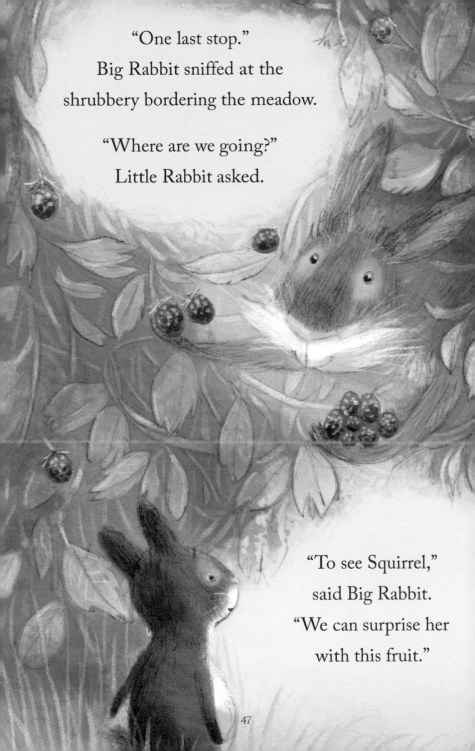

"One last stop."
Big Rabbit sniffed at the
shrubbery bordering the meadow.

"Where are we going?"
Little Rabbit asked.

"To see Squirrel,"
said Big Rabbit.
"We can surprise her
with this fruit."

The two rabbits bounded back across
the meadow towards the woodland,
heading straight for one of Little Rabbit's
favourite places – Squirrel's den.

As they neared the tree-trunk house,
Little Rabbit danced with excitement.
She loved visiting the Squirrels' home.

Squirrel was an amazing gymnast and was
full of stories of her tree-flying adventures.

So when Little Rabbit wriggled her way up through the tree into the squirrel den she was shocked to see her hero lying on a bed of leaves, her left leg tied to a twig. "What happened, Squirrel?" she cried.

"Little Rabbit, you won't believe
the story I have to tell you."

Squirrel told the rabbits about how
she had attempted to jump from her tree
to the neighbouring one.

"I landed perfectly but the branch gave way under my feet," Squirrel explained. "It must have rotted over the winter. I've sprained my paw."

She glanced at her family, biting her lip with worry. "I won't be able to collect food and the children are too young to forage for themselves."

Big Rabbit laid down the berries on the table. "I wish I'd known, Squirrel. We would've brought you more berries."

Poor Squirrels, Little Rabbit thought. The berries might last them today but what about tomorrow and the day after? She couldn't help but feel a little guilty about the delicious carrot dinner waiting for her at home.

53

The next morning, Little Rabbit woke early. She had a fluttery feeling in her chest from worrying about Granny Hedgehog, Mole, Squirrel and Dormouse all night long. She needed to talk to Big Rabbit right away.

"Where's Big Rabbit, Mama?" she asked.

"He left early this morning
to go on a walk," Mama said.
"But he told me to give you this."

She reached across the table and
picked up a small sheet of paper.

A task! Little Rabbit loved tasks.

To my very helpful assistant,
Please could you find me
the following important things;
Shiny paper
  Flowers
  Twigs

  Love,
    Big Rabbit

"Mama, I have to find some important
things for Big Rabbit," she said.
"Can I go outside?"

"So long as you stay near the warren," Mama
said. "But don't you want breakfast first—"

Before Mama could finish her sentence,
Little Rabbit raced out of the warren.

Outside in the meadow she looked at the list. The first thing she had to get was shiny paper.

Little Rabbit smiled. She had the piece from yesterday that she was saving for a kite. She looked at the list again: shiny paper, twigs and flowers… Suddenly it dawned on her – twigs and paper could only mean one thing … Big Rabbit was going to help her make her kite!

She fetched the shiny paper and moved
on to the next item – flowers.

Little Rabbit took a deep breath in as
she remembered jumping through the field
and smelling the sweet bluebells on the way
to visit Granny Hedgehog.

She scampered over to the meadow which
was bathed in sunshine. The wildflowers looked
like jewels dotted over a bright green canvas.
She scooped up a tiny bouquet and added
in some wild roses, too. Perhaps they would
decorate the kite string with the flowers.

The final item on the list was the twigs.
This was easy! Little Rabbit knew the best
spot for twigs, over in the woodland.

She hopped across and chose two of the
finest twigs she had ever seen. They would
be perfect for building a strong frame for her
kite. She picked up a few more
in case Big Rabbit wanted to
make his own kite.

Now all she had to do was find her
grandfather.

"There you are!" said a familiar voice.

Little Rabbit turned round to find her
grandfather coming back from his walk.

"I found all the things on the list,
Big Rabbit," she said excitedly.

"Great work! They're just what I need for my job today," he said, admiring all the things his granddaughter had collected. "Follow me."

A job? Little Rabbit's ears drooped. Perhaps she and Big Rabbit weren't making a kite, after all. She hopped slowly behind Big Rabbit, careful not to drop anything.

"What are we doing here?" Little Rabbit
asked as they headed over to the woods in
the direction of Mole's tunnel.

"You'll see," said Big Rabbit as he thumped
on the ground outside Mole's burrow.

Mole's familiar pink snout popped
up through the entrance and
Big Rabbit helped him out.

"Mole," Big Rabbit said. "I think we have solved your light problem."

He took the shiny paper and propped it up with a stick by the entrance to the tunnel.

"Little Rabbit, I hope you don't mind but I think your paper will help us all to see when we visit the Moles."

Little Rabbit's mouth fell open in surprise.
The shiny paper caught the sunlight and
reflected it down the tunnel.

"My goodness, Big Rabbit!" Mole exclaimed.
"You've done it! It's utterly brilliant."

Little Rabbit felt a warm feeling in her
tummy. Her kite paper meant Little Mole
could have his party!

"Thank you, Little Rabbit, for letting me
have your special paper," Mole cried.

Little Rabbit beamed in delight.

"But what about the twigs and the flowers?"
Little Rabbit asked as they left Mole's and
headed for the meadow.

"Aha! We'll need those in a moment,"
replied Big Rabbit.

As she raced across the field, Little Rabbit
spotted her friends, Little Hedgehog and
Little Mole, who were playing outside
Granny Hedgehog's nest.

"Will you hoppity hop with us, Little Rabbit?"
Little Mole said as she joined them.

"I'm helping Big Rabbit with a job at
the moment," she said proudly.

"Can we help, too?" Little Hedgehog asked.

"I don't see why not," said Big Rabbit.

Little Hedgehog let the rabbits into his
grandmother's home and at once
Little Rabbit knew why she had been
asked to collect the flowers. As soon as
Granny caught sight of the colourful
blooms, her face brightened.

"These are beautiful, Little Rabbit,"
she said, taking a deep whiff.
"What a brilliant idea to bring the
outside inside. I feel better already."

And suddenly Little Rabbit realized
what it was that her grandfather did.
He listened. And he helped.
And he made sure no one in their
community was ever forgotten.

"I think I know what these twigs
are for," Little Rabbit said to
Big Rabbit. "These are to help
Dormouse build a bigger nest."

"That's right," said Big Rabbit.
"I hope you aren't too disappointed
about the kite."

Little Rabbit had completely forgotten about the kite. She had been having too much fun helping everyone out.

"Of course not," she laughed. "These twigs are much better for building nests than making kites."

"And now we have some helpers to look after the dormice babies while Dormouse builds his nest," Big Rabbit said, nodding at Little Mole and Little Hedgehog.

Dormouse was overjoyed to see
the splendid twigs and his babies
couldn't wait to play with Little
Rabbit and her friends.

"Thank you for everything,
Big Rabbit," Dormouse said.
"And thank you, too, Little Rabbit,"
he smiled, shaking her paw.

Little Rabbit beamed. But there was someone who she couldn't stop thinking about. And the fluttery feeling of worry she had felt in her chest that morning was back.

"What about Squirrel, Big Rabbit?" she asked. "How will we help her? We don't have anything left."

Big Rabbit sighed. "I shall have to do my best. I can take her berries every day."

"What about the other chores?" said Little Rabbit. "Who will help clean the den? Or look after the squirrel babies?"

Big Rabbit scratched his chin.

"I'm not sure," he said.

Little Rabbit thought hard. "Big Rabbit,
I have an idea." She jumped up and
called everyone round her.

"What if all of us help Squirrel together?"
she said. "We could take turns to get food,
clean the den and look after the babies. If all
the neighbours join in then it won't be long
until Squirrel is up on her feet."

"That's a fantastic idea, Little Rabbit,"
Big Rabbit said, giving her a hug.

The warm feeling in Little Rabbit's
tummy started to grow while the fluttery
feeling in her chest faded away. As she
watched her friends and Dormouse talk
about helping Squirrel, she couldn't stop
the smile stretching across her face.

"I spy with my little eye,
something beginning with C,"
Big Rabbit whispered in
Little Rabbit's ear.

"Carrots?" Little Rabbit
suggested as Big Rabbit
pulled out a carrot from
the ground.

Little Rabbit's tummy began
to rumble. She'd been so busy
that morning that she'd quite
forgotten about breakfast.

"Try again," Big Rabbit said,
drawing her into a big hug.

"Cuddles?"

"You're getting closer,"
Big Rabbit said,
his eyes twinkling.

"Carroty cuddles?"

"You got it, Little Rabbit!"

Fin